LAST BUT NOT LEAST

by Michael Scotto

illustrated by The Ink Circle

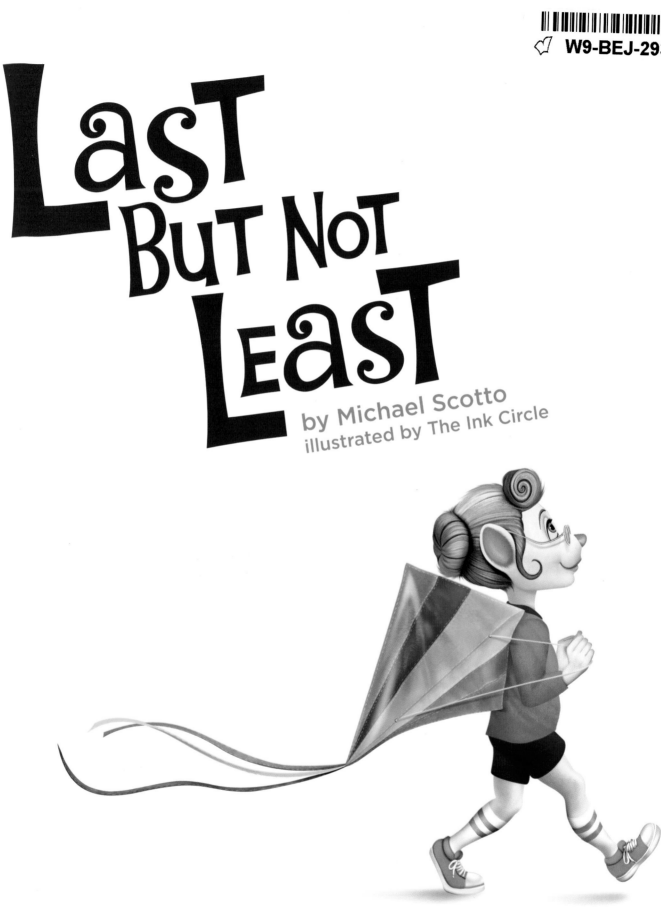

WELCOME TO MIDLANDIA

OUR STORY BEGINS

Midlandia University

Community Center

Animal Land

Town Square

HERE

Playland Park

Bike Factory

Harvest Farms

The Midlandia Summer Festival took place every year. Everyone in town got together to enjoy the sun, eat delicious food, and play games.

Sew loved the picnic. "The sky is perfect for kite flying!" she thought. Sew was a seamstress, and she had a special kite that she had stitched herself.

Sew loved nearly everything about the festival. Everything except...
"The games," she grumbled.

MIDLANDIA SUMMER FESTIVAL

It wasn't that Sew did not want to play. She wanted to play very much. "But when we split into teams, I always get picked last," Sew thought. "Being picked last just isn't any fun."

Still, Sew was willing to give the games another chance. "After all, Builda is captain of one of the kickball teams," Sew thought. Builda and Sew had become good friends over the last year. **"This time could be different."**

Sew waited with everyone as Builda and Brick picked their teams. "I'll take Sparky," Builda said. "I'll take Harvest," Brick said. **Sew began to get nervous.**

Soon, Sew was standing alone. "We have seven, and you have six," Brick told Builda. **"So you have to take Sew."**

Sew smiled. She was the last one picked, but at least she was on her friend's team. Builda looked at Sew. **"Um...that's okay,"** Builda said to Brick. "You go ahead and have one extra."

Sew was shocked! "But Builda..." she started. "Sorry, Sew," Builda replied. "I know we're buddies, but I play to win."

Coach, the referee, came and blew his whistle. "Builda!" he barked. "You need to have the same number on each team, or you can't play the game. **Go on over, Sew.**"

Brick snickered as Coach jogged away. "Yes!"
Brick said. "With Sew on the other team, there's no
way we can lose!" **Sew felt very embarrassed.**

"All right," Builda told her team. "We can still win this game, even with Sew on our side."

"I'm not that bad, everybody," Sew protested. "I might not be the fastest, or the best thrower—"

"When we played horseshoes last year," Builda interrupted, "you broke every window in the community center!" **The whole team laughed.**

Sew had had enough. "If you're going to laugh at me," she said, "then I'll just go fly my kite." "**No, wait!**" Builda called out. But Sew had already left the field.

Sew's kite glided through the air. She preferred to fly kites with friends, but everyone else was still at the Summer Festival. "At least I have the sky all to myself," Sew thought. Then, she heard a voice behind her.

"It must be lonely to fly that kite all alone," Coach said. **"It's better than being laughed at,"** Sew replied.

Coach sat down beside Sew. "I've already spoken with Builda and everyone else," he said. "They should not have been making fun."

"Yes, they should have! **I'm terrible at sports**," Sew said. "I never wanted to play, anyway."

"Is that really true?" Coach asked. "No," Sew huffed. "It's okay if you aren't very good at kickball," Coach said. "That's no reason to stop trying. **Nobody is good at everything.**"

"I don't feel like I'm good at anything, Coach," Sew said. **"I can't run fast...**

...or jump high...

...and when the ball comes to me, I get really nervous and **I miss it."**

"There are plenty of other things you are great at," Coach said. "You sew wonderful clothes. And look up in the sky. You might not be able to jump very high, but the kite you made soars higher than any other in Midlandia."

Sew blushed. "Really?" "The next time I need a new kite, you'll be the first Midlandian I talk to!" Coach declared. **"Thanks, Coach,"** Sew said. "That makes me feel better."

"I know getting picked last can hurt your feelings. Just remember that **last does not always mean least,"** Coach told her. "Do you think you can give kickball another chance?"

Sew returned to the kickball field. "We're sorry for giving you a hard time," Builda told her. "It was not very nice of us," Brick added. "I forgive you," Sew said. **"Let's play ball!"**

Coach blew his whistle and the game began. After everyone had played for a while, it was finally Sew's turn at the plate. "All right, Sew, you're the last one to kick," Builda said.

Sew was excited to get a chance, but she was nervous, too. "What if I miss the ball and ruin the game?" she thought. Then Sew spotted Coach on the sidelines. **"Last is not least!"** he shouted.

Sew knew that **Coach was right**.
As Brick rolled the kickball toward her, Sew stopped worrying. She just ran forward and gave the **best kick** she could. As it turned out, Sew's best was more than good enough.

DISCUSSION QUESTIONS

In this story, Sew is picked last to play kickball.
Was there ever a time you felt left out of an activity?

How did you handle it?